Charlotte Zolotow

THIS QUIET LADY

Pictures by
Anita Lobel

(Greenwillow Books) 1992
N E W   Y O R K

Watercolor and gouache paints were used for
the full-color art. The text type is ITC Esprit Medium.

Printed in Singapore by Tien Wah Press
First Edition
1   2   3   4   5   6   7   8   9   10

Library of Congress Cataloging-in-Publication Data

Zolotow, Charlotte (date)
This quiet lady / by Charlotte Zolotow ; pictures by Anita Lobel.
p.   cm.
Summary: A child finds out about her mother's early life by
looking at old pictures.
ISBN 0-688-09305-1.   ISBN 0-688-09306-X (lib. bdg.)
[1. Mothers — Fiction.]   I. Lobel, Anita, ill.
II. Title.   PZ7.Z77Qe   1992
[E] — dc20   90-38485   CIP   AC

For Charlotte Kate Turner, with love —C. Z.

For my daughter, Adrianne, with love —A. L.

This baby
smiling in her bassinette
under the crocheted throw
is my mother.

This curly-haired little girl
with the doll
drooping from her hand
is my mother.

This untidy schoolgirl
with her wrinkled stockings
is my mother.

This young lady
laughing with those boys
is my mother.

This girl with long dark hair
and dark eyes
dressed in a cap and gown
is my mother.

This bride
like a white flower
is my mother.

This young woman
with my father's arm around her
is my mother.

This quiet lady,
lovely and large,
standing on our front porch
is my mother.

And here is where I begin.

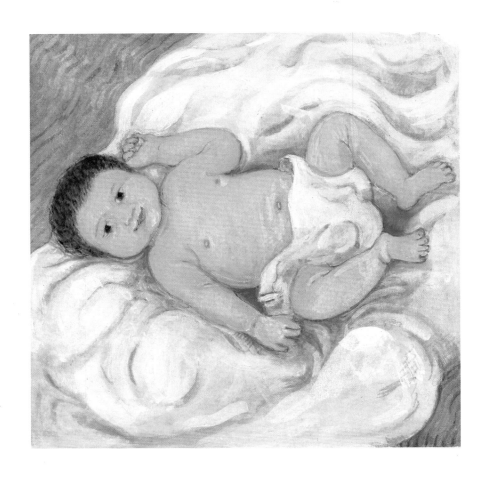

The Beginning